THE
SECRET
OF
MUSIC

The Secret of Music

a look at the listening life

Joshua McGuire

Shanti Arts Publishing
Brunswick, Maine

THE SECRET OF MUSIC
A Look at the Listening Life

Published by Shanti Arts Publishing

Interior and cover design by Shanti Arts Designs

Shanti Arts LLC
193 Hillside Road
Brunswick, Maine 04011

shantiarts.com

Cover image by ad_krikorian / istockphoto.com / 498661030
Interior image by cattallina / istockphoto.com / 892830170

Printed in the United States of America

ISBN: 978-1-947067-77-6 (softcover)
ISBN: 978-1-947067-78-3 (digital)

Library of Congress Control Number: 2019933163

For Jerry Howell.
Sitting among your books and records,
the lines began to blur.

CONTENTS

Sie ist um uns herum, sie ist auch in in uns drinnen.
In den Gesichtern rieselt sie, im Spiegel da rieselt sie,
in meinem Schläfen fließt sie.
Und zwischen mir und dir, da fließt sie wieder,
lautlos, wie eine Sanduhr.
Oh, Quinquin!
Manchmal hör' ich sie fließen — unaufhaltsam.
Manchmal steh' ich auf mitten in der Nacht
und lass die Uhren alle, alle stehn.
Allein man muß sich auch vor ihr nicht fürchten.

It is all around us, and it is inside us.
It trickles over our faces, it trickles over the mirror,
it flows between my temples.
And between you and me it flows once more,
silently, like an hourglass.
Oh Quinquin!
Sometimes I hear it flowing — ceaselessly.
Sometimes I rise in the middle of the night,
and stop all the clocks.
But we must not dread it.

> — Hugo von Hofmannsthal,
>   *Der Rosenkavalier*, Act I

PREFACE

THIS SHORT BOOK IS AN ADAPTATION OF SEVERAL talks given at Vanderbilt University from 2008–2012. The urge to wrestle lectures into book form may always be a misguided one, as it often results in writing that is at once too colloquial and too obscure. Moreover, the subject matter of these particular talks — listening to music — was slippery to begin with, for no one can listen to music while someone else is talking about listening to music.

Thus I want to emphasize that this book is not exactly a book — or at least it does not set out to succeed on a book's terms — and while I have included footnotes to give credit where credit is due, it is a book that makes no pretense to scholarship of any kind.

It is a collection of conjectures, offered from one lover of music to another.

Joshua McGuire

I. EXPERIENCE

AN INVITATION TO THE DANCE

THERE IS A SAYING THAT GETS PASSED AROUND in musical circles: "Talking about music is like dancing about architecture."[1] And I would like to begin by admitting this obvious truth: talking about music is impossible. Music itself — the sounding event in the air and the recognition of that event somewhere inside our bodies — is what it is. Music only ever exists in its own moment and in the experience of itself. Words can add nothing to it, and words can take nothing from it. Talking about music is not music. The art of talking is as separate from the art of music as dancing is from architecture. And yet I am willing to bet that you have had at least one experience with music you'd like to talk about.

When a really powerful listening experience comes over you, nothing in the world seems more important. Something in the music stops your breath, and suddenly there is nothing left in you but a sense of wordless truth.

---

1. It seems that no one knows who said it first; I have seen it attributed to Steve Martin, Elvis Costello, and Martin Mull.

You can't tell if that sense of truth is coming from outside you or inside you. Even if you've never heard the music before, it seems as if you know the next note before it sounds. Everything feels blindingly new, yet at the same time you have the uncanny feeling that you've been here before.

What is this fleeting experience that sometimes hits us when we listen to music? Why have we humans always insisted on having that experience? Amid sickness, war, poverty, and death, why do we return again and again to something so fundamentally useless as music: sound waves, invisible, untouchable, here and then gone?

Ultimately, only your individual experience of music can answer that question. You and I, therefore, have a simple but difficult job to do: we must constantly remember the difference between reality and representation. When I talk about listening to music, my description of listening is obviously just representation. But I am also counting on you to remember the reality, the direct experience of music in your own life. I am counting on you to find out what that experience is and to try it out again and again. Just talking about it does no good. The only thing that matters is the quality of experience you are getting from music.

So this book is more like a jumping-off point, an invitation to try a more complete kind of musical listening. Just talking about listening is like sitting on the couch at home, fully clothed, looking at photos of your beach vacation. It's all well and good — and we all enjoy looking at photos — but listening is actually being at the beach. Listening is the sand on your skin, the glittering heaves of green water, the tipsy smell of sunlight in the wind.

Sadly, however, we can only ever traffic in symbols of that direct listening experience. Some people talk about what music does to our brain waves; others talk about what kind of chord they see written on the page; and everyone can talk about how they feel when they listen to music, or what city they were living in when they discovered their favorite band.

In other words, we can talk about ourselves and our own history and our own perceptions all day long, and these are certainly worthwhile things to talk about. But we can never quite put our finger on the living spark that fires in the moment between the music and us. In the moment of true and total listening, we are by definition knocked speechless.

So any attempt to be "objective" about music's effect on us — in other words, to treat our own brain or music's structure as an object of study — comes up short because music happens between subject and object. It is a quality of space between things, and as an experience, it cannot be preserved. Yet it always leaves its residue in us after the fact, and we can only ever talk about the residue.

You might say that all our words about music — and for that matter all our thoughts and feelings about music, all our recordings and scores and instruments and rehearsals and concert tickets, and everything else that we normally think of as "music" — are like the muddy paw print my basset hound leaves on the carpet in our den. By the time I walk in the den to find the paw print, the culprit hound has disappeared. Now I could stay and analyze and discuss the exact nature of that paw print all afternoon, but music is the living and vanished dog. This book is an attempt to say something about the dog itself, about music, the untraceable experience in time. It will only work if you remember an important experience with music from your own life.

You know perfectly well what I am talking about: when you listen to music, a sense of freshness sometimes comes over you. It is as if you are remembering a secret you had forgotten. Music finds a place inside you where there is no difference between joy and pain.

Now if you have never, ever felt anything like this while listening to music, you should probably put this book down. You should go listen to more music. But if you have even the slightest inkling of the experience I'm talking about — the experience in which music overwhelms you — read on. Your experience is something that can be expanded and amplified. No matter how deep it seems, this kind of listening can always be deepened.

◆

ANOTHER WAY OF SAYING ALL THIS IS THAT MUSIC beckons us toward complete involvement in our experience. "Complete involvement in our experience" sounds like great fun, but the truth is we often resist it because complete involvement means we cannot document the experience in any way. If we try to capture an experience while we are in the middle of it, we remove ourselves from it.

We see this catch-22 every day on social media. Someone posts, "Enjoying an excellent meal with my beautiful wife." And, of course, if we're in our right mind, we realize that this person is actually *not* enjoying an excellent meal with his beautiful wife. He's actually typing on his phone.

It is a terrible paradox, and we have all been caught in it. The attempt to capture life cuts us off from life. Complete involvement requires real courage because to be completely involved we must consent to preserve nothing of our experience. In the moment, complete involvement doesn't even know that it is complete involvement. It cannot describe itself midstream. The experience is the butterfly; the word is the needle.

The beauty of music is that it can forcefully pull us into this kind of complete involvement before we realize what's happening and comment on it and ruin it. Music sometimes yanks us by the collar and gives us the chance to enter into unguarded contact with a white-hot part of our experience that, in common hours, we aren't even aware exists.

Though we have all had brief flashes of it, this vivid kind of listening is still rare for most of us. We have a natural tendency to avoid the intensity of such complete listening, and we unconsciously use our everyday habits to cover it up. There are times when the response we want to have to music seems too much, too powerful to bear. We feel we might lose ourselves in it. So we treat all music as background music.

But if we can articulate something of what good listening is and how it works, we can use it to amplify our daily experience. We can sustain it. This is worth the effort, for listening to music in a fuller way shows us a fuller way to live.

This fuller way to live is not about having "good

taste" or "culture," or my trying to sell you on the relative merits of classical music. I simply mean that the act of listening — to any kind of music at all — clarifies the way we listen to everything. It is as though, somewhere along the way, we all lost the courage to listen completely to other people, to the world around us, and to the passage of our own lives. Music, in moments, restores that courage. So the first thing we can say about music — this force that possesses us with a savage vulnerability, makes us fight, makes us love, and seems to make the dead speak again — is that it always invites us more fully into life.

BROKEN CLOCKS

"This is this. This ain't something else. THIS is THIS."

THIS LINE, WHICH MUST BE MY FAVORITE IN ALL film, is spoken by Robert DeNiro's character, Mike, in the 1978 movie *The Deer Hunter*. Mike isn't referring to anything in particular. It is a clear day, and he is sitting atop his car on the side of a mountain where he and a group of friends are about to go hunting. Mike's friend Stan, played by John Cazale, has forgotten his hunting boots and has asked to borrow Mike's. "No . . ." says Mike, chiding Stan for his inattention, "THIS is THIS."

Stan dismisses Mike's tautology as "some faggot-sounding bullshit." Mike, without any further comment, fires his rifle into the empty air.

◆

WHENEVER I HEAR AN EFFECTIVE PIECE OF music — music that really does what it sets out to do — I often resort to DeNiro's line to describe what the experience was like: THIS is THIS. I think it comes as close as we can come in words to articulating the realization that dawns on us when we hear great music. A great piece of music is itself. A great piece of music screams, "THIS is THIS." Nothing more can be added to the unutterable "THIS." When we are close to this naked presence in music, we can never pin down exactly what is being done to us. The experience holds us fast, even though the keenness of it isn't exactly pleasant. Good listening is like grabbing a live wire, the shock of which renders you unable to let go of the live wire.

When this bare charge of music hits us, there is often a tremendous emotional effect as well. But we should notice that the real activity of music — its "THIS-ness," if you will[2] — exists with or without our emotional response to it. We may feel sad, or excited, or resolute, or a thousand other things as we listen to music, but to say so is a statement about ourselves, not about music. The space music opens in us allows us to feel our own emotions more strongly. But we can clearly see that music is not those emotions. Nor does music "contain" those emotions in the usual sense of that word.

Anyone who has ever written music knows this to be true. Whatever emotions you pour into your music as you compose it are not necessarily the emotions people take away from listening to it. Expecting everyone to get your specific emotion from your specific piece of music is like putting one red ticket into a hopper full of white tickets, then expecting everyone who walks into the room to draw a red one. Once the music sounds, its composer is

---

2. To allude not only to Robert DeNiro but also to Meister Eckhart: *isticheit* or "is-ness" as the ground of being.

no more in control of its emotional effect on people than anyone else.

Take, for example, a relatively well-known piece of classical music: the slow movement from Beethoven's Symphony No. 7. This piece is used to very good effect in the movie *Mr. Holland's Opus*. Mr. Holland, the music teacher played by Richard Dreyfuss, is explaining to his students that Beethoven was deaf and is playing a recording of the slow movement from the Seventh Symphony while he speaks. In a previous scene, we have seen that Mr. Holland's son was born deaf. And so, as this rather serious and somber-sounding music plays, we think, "Wow, Beethoven was deaf, Mr. Holland's son is deaf, this sad-sounding music is about sorrow over deafness. Aha!" And in that moment we naïvely feel that we have decoded the emotional "message" of the music.

But then again, I had a friend in college who, whenever she heard the slow movement from the Seventh, became sexually aroused. I had a teacher who wept with quiet joy whenever she conducted it. If you have ever seen the movie *The King's Speech*, you have heard this music used — and it seems very appropriate in the moment — to accompany a declaration of world war. And if we go to the music itself, on the page, Beethoven marked that it should be played *allegretto* — not slow or sad at all, but rather "a little fast." (The root word in Italian, *allegro*, literally means "cheerful.") So while listening to music may certainly be emotional for us, music itself is something other than our emotion. Music exists prior to any private emotional reactions it may cause in us, and there are as many different emotional reactions to a piece of music as there are people listening to it.

In other words, contrary to popular superstition, music does not inject a separate substance called "soul" or "heart" or "feeling" into us like a metaphysical syringe. The power of music abides somewhere else, somewhere beyond the chemical vagary of our emotions; music is more like a canvas on which they become visible, or a space through which they pass. What happens to us when this space gets opened up and emotions we could never explain to anyone else suddenly pour through it? How does music do this to us? What can we say, specifically, about that sense of spaciousness that sometimes comes in listening?

It is easier to speak specifically about what it is if we consider other situations in which it sometimes arises. Do you ever notice, for instance, what happens to your sense of time in airports or hospitals? Someone you have seen a thousand times before is there, and you say goodbye to them for the thousandth time. But this time, as you turn and lose yourself in the crowd, something draws you completely into the texture of that moment. Everything else goes silent. You know, very clearly, that this could be the last time you ever see that person. The shocking thing is not this realization, but the fact that you never realized it before; of course, this could be the last time. It could always be the last time. Why do I not hang on to this knowledge all the time?

Or perhaps it comes to you while traveling. After racing to see all the famous sights in a new city, you accidentally come upon some empty cathedral or park at sunset. For no reason, the rug gets jerked out from under you. In an instant, there is the sense not only that you've been here before, but also that everything else — this whole trip, the year before it, the crushing hours wasted at your job, the last three girlfriends, your whole childhood — everything was just as it was for the purpose of bringing you to the old newness of this precise place at this precise moment. All the mistakes were perfect because they brought you here. The logic of clock-and-calendar time falls away. In an instant, you see past the grating hours and minutes into a web of cause and effect you had missed before. You see that your usual way of thinking about time is all wrong.

When it comes to music, the sense of skewed time is almost a cliché: "I heard such-and-such a song, and suddenly I was back there again . . . " But what I'm talking about here is not just the associative tipping off of forgotten memories. I'm talking about a shift in our awareness of time itself. As we listen to music, we sometimes have an altered sense of time — the sense inside a song at a wedding, or a funeral, or during an everyday commute — time bent back on itself, of events separated by decades suddenly coexisting. Lacking a word for it, the French composer Olivier Messiaen borrowed an Indian word to describe the phenomenon in his music: *turangalîla*, or "time-play." You notice that your life really is passing by, yet it is also standing still. You have the sense that a persistent illusion has fallen away, and for the first time once again, you are seeing things as they are.

If we would admit it, we all know this experience. At some point, music has, as it spun its own time in the air, pushed us over into a place beyond chronology, a place where the past seems near again, and the future seems blissfully unimportant. It is also a place literally beyond ourselves in that it is beyond our own persistent mental concept of who we are; that is, a self measured by clock-time. Even a little taste of this loss of self is enough to animate long stretches of ordinary life. Perhaps if you have experienced it, you have kept it to yourself, hidden the tears it sometimes brings, or covered it with the soft noise of distraction.

It is not an emotion but rather a heightened awareness. It cuts through our usual boredom into the realization that THIS moment is most urgently THIS moment. There will never, ever, ever be another one, and at every moment of your life, that statement is always true.

This suddenly clear perception of the strangeness of time — or what we might call the vertical quality of time when its usual horizontal flow is disrupted — is something music can always give us. It is felt as a sharper, crisper aliveness. Of course, we have to participate fully as listeners in order to step over into that aliveness, and we are very good at pulling back. Yet I think you know, in your own experience with music, what I'm talking about. You know that at its best, music is not simply an entertainment to distract us during our break time.

Music is here to break time.

TIME AFTER TIME

W E SPEND OUR TIME LISTENING TO MUSIC, AND, in turn, music gives us an altered sense of time.

It is easy to brush over that first phrase without realizing what it means: "We spend our time listening to music . . . " Listening to music, in other words, costs us time. Listen to five minutes of music, and you're five minutes closer to death.

Perhaps this is why our feelings about music earn the dubious name "passionate" (from the Latin root meaning "to suffer"). Show someone a painting that disgusts or bores them, and they can just keep walking through the gallery. Play them a piece of music they hate, and the emotional temperature runs a little higher because a section of their life, which they will never get back, has been spent listening to it.

Conversely, when you hear great music, it is this passage of time, this sacrifice of part of yourself that makes the listening "passionate." Passion is a suffering joy. Listening to music you love is not gaining an emotion of joy, like popping a drug; it is actually giving something up. In listening, an exchange of time takes place between you and music. Think of the first time you heard your favorite piece of music, and the clock seemed to stop. In that passionate exchange, what is being given, and what is being gained? You are giving music a complete section of your usual clock-time, and music is giving you its strange, re-measured time in return.

Think of it like this: you cannot listen to music without beginning to listen and, at some point, ceasing to listen. This means we can imagine any listening experience as a unique section of time with a fixed beginning and end, a patch of your life consumed by listening,[3] a part of your own time that becomes inseparable from the time of the music. Your time and the music's time fuse to form a unique entity, book-ended by the music's beginning and end. Apart from this living, timed experience of listening, music has no substantial existence.

And this is the primal power of music: when you hand over a section of your own life to listening, music can re-structure the way you experience your life. In listening to music, you exchange a bit of time that would have passed by unnoticed for time consciously spent. Music gives us the sound of time passing. In other words, music gives us life.

And, of course, music has a fixed endpoint in time. Listening to music can be such a shattering experience precisely because this bounded-in-time quality is something we rigidly ignore about our own lives.

---

3. See John Rahn's essay, "Repetition," in *Music Inside Out: Going too Far in Musical Essays* (Amsterdam: G+B Arts International, 2001) for a fascinating model of repetition vis à vis the section of a listener's life "lived alongside" the music.

Unconsciously, we assume that our lives are not bounded in time and that we will always have another day. We keep our own death hidden from view, and we refuse to conceive of our lives as finite units of time. But listening to music forces us to experience a complete unit of time — begun and ended — in miniature.[4] In music, we get a feeling for what the whole thing could be like. The limitedness of it mirrors to us the shocking truth that our own time is limited too. A piece of music is a microcosm of our whole life, sewn down into the fabric of that life. With each note that passes, there is less and less music to be heard; just as with each note that passes, there is less and less of our experience to be lived. Music forces us to face the music.

When we hear the unstoppability of time's passing, we encounter something that goes deeper than passing feelings. We encounter a structural change in the way we know ourselves. We finally see the dagger's glint, the real danger in being alive that we almost always miss. Music serves as a *memento mori*, a reminder of death. It makes us brave enough to face the irreplaceable quality of each day. If we know that the music is drawing to an end right now and that we will only hear it once, we listen for all we're worth.

By flashing our awareness back in on itself, music delivers us into ecstasy (from the Greek *ex stasis*, a "standing-outside-of" our own lives). We stand beside ourselves in listening, and listen to a section of our own time vanish. The usual scrim of dullness is torn away. As the needle drops, as the bow is drawn, all music shouts

---

4. See Rahn, pp. 17–18.

in our ears the urgent news that this note, this phrase, this hour is always coming steadily closer, closer to its own end. All music says, "Pay attention!" "This will not last forever!" "Are you catching this?" By reminding us that we are dying, music reminds us that we are alive. It returns us to an utter simplicity of perception and destroys time by drawing that perception so completely into the present moment that we sometimes wake from the hideous dream of a fixed past or an ephemeral future. We sense the stillness of the one thing that has always been with us: the presence of this present instant. And in that instant, music is forever speaking its silent truth: NOW is NOW.

When we taste this awareness of the fact that we are aware, we cannot hang onto it for long. We pull back from the shining realm of paradox where loss is gain and joy hurts, and return to the four walls around us. The stark consciousness of the fact that we are conscious at all seems too beautiful to bear. We avert our eyes from this relentless gaze and retreat again into a world of bloodless memory and timid planning. "Go, go, go . . . " says the bird in Eliot's *Four Quartets*, " . . . human kind cannot bear very much reality."

No matter. For this apparent departure from the statistical norm, this world that we glimpse when music burns away the fog of our mind, *is* reality. The urgency we perceive in music is true; that urgency is what time actually is, whether we feel it passing by or not. So listening to music is not about having the occasionally altered experience of reality. It is about recognizing, quite soberly, that music gives us the unaltered reality.

It is difficult to give ourselves so completely to reality

because doing so requires that we face a profound fear. That fear, like music, is made of time. We have all, in some way, been injured by time; we know that for anything we can possibly do, we can do it only a limited number of times. Each time we greet a friend, each time we visit a favorite city, we spend down one of those encounters. We burn a page of the book, never to be read again. And so to be completely open to the experience of life is also to admit our own mortality. The two go hand in hand. Our limitedness in time is the source of all our restlessness; but it is also, if we will turn and face it, the source of all our greatness.

Often, rather than face it, we try covering it over with drugs, unhealthy relationships, and mindless work. Or at best, we hide in the imaginary safety of the future. Like Hamlet, we fritter our lives away planning our lives. We never quite find the energy to get started. We fail to do the things we truly want to do because we imagine that we have more time.

We actually have less time. Each day, our experience of the world becomes a little narrower, for it becomes whatever we chose and ceases to be all that we did not choose. Music shows us this painful truth and so pushes us to do what we are meant to do and become what we are meant to become. In music there is no protection from life's passing. Normally we try to shield ourselves and act as though we could stand apart from the passage of time. We hesitate, we deliberate, we pause to reconsider. And in that moment of hesitation, all is lost. In music there is no hesitation because music is always in time with itself.

So listening to music, finally, is not about listening to

music. It is about listening to our own existence. We hear, therefore we are.

And what is the quality of that hearing? What was it she was wearing the first time you met? What exactly was it he said to you as he hung up the phone the last time you talked? Did you catch it? Will this be the last time?

Music asks us to ask that question every time.

♦

IF YOU CAN HOLD UP UNDER THE INTENSITY OF BEING realistic about time, if you can push on every minute for what it really is — possibly the last minute — you eventually stop chasing your life as if it were something out in front of you, something yet to be attained. Most of us behave as if that were the case; as if, like Pinocchio, we have yet to become a real person. We strain forward in our imagined timeline of plans, sure that the next diploma, the next job, the next city, the next marriage, our teacher's approval, our colleagues' admiration will somehow add up to the truth of who we are. One day, when we are grown up, we will do what we want.

We refuse to admit that we do not know, and have never known, what is going to happen to us from hour to hour. We don't even know from minute to minute. But to live perpetually on the edge of the complete unknown, to live truthfully, to admit we have no idea what will happen five minutes from now is too much for most people, and so they retreat into eager beliefs and fantasies about the future. This habit of placing responsibility for ourselves out into a completely imaginary dimension of time numbs us to the possibilities of our actual life.

Where is that actual life? We try to find it in the present moment. Yet we run into trouble because we think of the present moment as a knife blade slicing through time. Immeasurably thin, it cuts forward out of the past and into the future. But as for the present moment, we can't find it or hang onto it for long; it is too narrow, too fast, too fleeting.

In reality, just the opposite is true. The present moment is the one thing that never moves. Structurally, it is the one thing we can never escape. It is always here. It sits fixed, like an enormous mountain, and we have always been sitting on it. Over it, the events we call past and future drift like clouds.

The freedom you feel in music is the freedom to give your attention solely to what is happening right now. Whatever that is, it is the only thing that is ever happening. And whatever you know you must do with yourself, you are free to do it now. In fact, you can only ever do it now.

At first, it is hard work to remember this obvious truth: we are at all times completely alive, and life is not something doled out to us in more or less quantity at different times. Our own perception of life in the present instant — the only place in which we ever perceive anything — ceaselessly determines how much or how little life we imagine we are living. But the whole thing, the totality that we tend to grasp only in flashes, is always with us. Music helps us remember this, for music can only ever happen now.

II. IMPLICATIONS

THE LISTENING LIFE

L ET'S TAKE A CLOSER LOOK NOW AT HOW WE interact with music on a daily basis. What are some practical ways in which you might get more out of your own listening? No two people have the exact same relationship to music, so all attempts to talk about your listening life will be provisional. But what follows is a sketch of some basic principles I have found to be true for me.

Let me first say that as I write this, I have access, without leaving my seat, to two e-mail accounts, a social media messaging app, two video chat apps, and a smartphone. Much has been made in recent years of our connectivity, and I have no desire to throw more fuel on that fire. The general consensus on being connected seems to be that no one exactly likes it, but no one is willing to stop it either.

I would only like to point out that without leaving my seat, I can contact almost any living person I have ever known, no matter where they are on the planet. And I would like to point out the relationship between the obvious comfort such connectivity provides and the somewhat less obvious awareness we relinquish in exchange for it.

Since we are able to be in contact with virtually anyone in any moment, when we do meet someone face-to-face, we tend to miss the true thrust of who they are. Our consciousness of them as real people is diluted by the little representations we have of them via our technology. And so we have a sliding scale, whereby connectivity is gained and quality of attention is lost. No distance on Earth seems very great any more, making the distance between individuals very great indeed. Being "in touch" with everyone means that we never really touch anyone with our fullest possible attention.

To state it another way: we tend to ignore the pain inherent in meeting another person. To meet another person is to consent to have a final conversation with that person. It will happen; there is no way around it. But being constantly able to have a conversation with them renders us numb to this fact.

The point is not that we ought to give up our communication technology, but simply that we should see the relationship between silence and meaning. This relationship is the moral of the story in Aesop's fable, "The Boy Who Cried Wolf." Less communication is more, and more is less. We forget this principle in the moment of contact with others, however, because underneath our demand for constant connectivity lies *timor mortis*, the fear of death.

We can see this fear plainly in our own experience. Those of us who remember driving before cell phones know that once you were out on a trip, you were out of touch unless something went wrong and you had to use a pay phone. Now, if a driver runs late and doesn't call, we fear them dead within half an hour. Our habitual tiny strokes of communication, once they are removed, reveal anxiety. This is not to say that technology causes anxiety; to say so would be essentially superstitious. Perhaps communication technology is rather a parallel symptom of our anxiety, or a kind of symbol for it. More precisely: technology's absence forms a window into an anxiety that has always been with us. Using constant communication to cover up that anxiety is simply the mechanism of addiction.

The alternative to such addiction is silence. There are two kinds of silence. The first kind, which everyone finds excruciating, is forced silence, the kind you get by not calling someone or not opening up the computer when you really, really want to (in which case the inside of your head is actually not silent at all, but rather noisy). The second kind of silence, which most people never reach because they can't sit through the first kind long enough, is true silence, which bubbles up from the state of not knowing something and then releasing the need to know. In that true silence, there is a profound self-sufficiency. It is the background field on which your life plays out, the blank canvas on which a million otherwise unrelated events are painted. In that silence, you see that no one conversation is ever all-important, and yet you see that each conversation is perfectly unique, and therefore all-important.

And so, if the compulsive use of communication technology covers up this refreshing silence, we can learn to handle it lightly. We can learn to participate in each face-to-face interaction fully, tasting it as a singular and unrepeatable event. We can accept the exciting vigor of the silences in between the conversations.

Likewise, as listeners, we can learn not to dilute the power of musical communication by attempting to experience music constantly. The simple fact that we can experience music constantly makes it difficult not to do so, for who wouldn't want to hear more music? Yet silence, like it or not, is the ground of musical attention. No art museum hangs paintings on a wall already busy with colors and designs. Good museums hang paintings on a clean, white wall that draws no attention to itself and doesn't compete with the artwork. In the same way, silence is the empty background field on which a piece of music must be presented if we are to have a chance at quality listening. If there is too much music, we will never hear any music. To understand music's subtler messages, we have to be soaked in silence. Yet we happen to live in an era that fears silence immensely.

Perhaps because of our fear of silence, we usually end up listening to music passively. To listen passively means that some music, which we did not choose ourselves, is taking place in the background while other things are going on. I am suggesting that we can also listen actively. Now on the one hand, listening passively is harmless enough; I do it every day when I step into a restaurant, a waiting room, or an elevator. To some extent it is unavoidable. But if listening passively is our only way of listening, we are training a habit of mind that is literally dangerous.

If we are willing to lay back and halfway listen to whatever comes down the musical pike — without really choosing it and interacting with it in some way, or at least trying to articulate why we love it or hate it — then we may be just as willing to float down the stream of whatever happens, in a state of distraction, until one day we wake up in a miserable job or a hateful relationship that we never really chose either. And this is, in fact, how most people live out their lives — passively.

But music, since it surrounds us at every turn, gives us an opportunity to practice the opposite habit of mind. When we consistently turn a fierce attention outward on something as ineffable as music, we develop clarity about other important aspects of our being that usually go unnoticed too. We learn to be actively alert, rather than alert only when we are forced to be by means of joy or pain. Music prepares us to be alert enough to guide our own existence instead of being guided by it.

So let us proceed with the understanding that how we listen to music can affect much more than how we listen to music. Our *listening* life — the time that we spend listening to music — can actually lead to a listening *life*. It can lead to the kind of life that listens to itself, and in turn understands and actively chooses its own place in the world.

♦

IN ORDER TO EXPAND OUR EAR ENOUGH TO TASTE THE fullness of musical sound, we do not have to do anything. To expand our ear, we only have to stop doing things.

Doctors tell us that we stand a much better chance of eating a healthy diet if we do not take our meals while attempting to do other things. And we know from experience that we get more flavor out of our food if we approach it single-mindedly and do not mix the act of eating with other distractions. This is why a person can polish off a whole pound of chicken wings at Hooter's. You don't exactly notice the flavor or the fact that you've finished a whole plate because you're not paying attention to the wings. By contrast, if you go to a five-star restaurant, you wake up and pay attention to each bit of food as it comes. In that room, a small slice of meat is enough to fill you up. You pause, and you understand not only how filling and delicious this particular bite of food is, but also how stunning it is that food exists at all. Sometimes you see, as if for the first time, that *food is food*. Thanks in part to this better food, but also thanks to the better environment, you eat, and you know that you are eating.

Listening to music is no different. But when it comes to music, thanks to our excellent abundance of it, we are usually on the Hooter's plan. Music becomes just another part of the whole experience. Music is playing, but we aren't cognizant of the fact that we are listening to music.

To improve our listening, then, is to get more pleasure out of listening. The more the ear opens, the more it can take in and the more it can enjoy. What follows is an illustration of how that opening might take place in your daily routine. Bear in mind this is just an illustration, and it is useless unless you try it out for yourself.[5]

The next time you drive your car or ride public transit somewhere alone, notice the compulsion to put on some music as soon as you get seated. Just for today, let that compulsion go. Make your morning commute

---

5. See also W. A. Mathieu, *The Listening Book: Discovering Your Own Music* (Boston: Shambhala, 1991).

with no music, no talk radio, no phone calls, nothing. As you travel, you will probably notice that the chatter in your head — that imaginary mental conversation we are always carrying on — seems louder. Hearing this chatter is grating; that's why we usually cover it up with music. Leave the music off anyway. For now, the mental chatter is going to be your soundtrack. Notice it. You don't really get to decide what comes down the stream of consciousness next, so just observe it for a moment. Watch it ramble and twist.

Then, place your ear on something else, something outside yourself. What is the difference, for instance, between the sound of the engine, the sound of the wheels, and the sound of the wind as the vehicle cuts through it? Can you locate each one? Place your attention on each one separately for a moment. What is happening, physically, with each sound?

Is it going up or down in pitch? Is one higher or lower than another? Is there a regular beat inside any of these three sounds? If there is a pulse in more than one, and do they ever line up? What is the tone of each sound like? What about its texture? What adjective would you use to describe it? Which sound is loudest? Which is softest? Does the volume change? Now notice other sounds inside and outside the vehicle. Expand the field of your hearing without losing the original three sounds. What else do you hear?

This placing of attention on things you normally block out opens the ear, and anyone can do it at any time. You don't have to know any technically correct musical labels to do it. It is simply a loosening of the ear's attention, the relaxing of an aperture that we usually keep closed. It is not a matter of talent or of special training, but this relaxing is ninety percent of what "having a good ear" actually is. Many professional musicians never do it. Perhaps this is because of a terrible paradox: in order to open the ear to music, we must temporarily get rid of music.

As you go about the day at your destination, remember to keep some of this open attention on the sound of the room you're in. Still, if possible, avoid music. If you're at work, notice the sounds of your work instead. What is the tone of this tool versus that one when you set it down? What kind of paper makes the best sound when it comes up from your desk? What is the tone of the ticks coming from the clock? What is the difference between the sound of the ductwork and the sound of the light bulbs? Notice everything. Notice that if you fail to notice something, it's not because you lack some magical skill; it's just that you don't remember to do it.

Now, for the return trip home. Begin in the same way. Get in the vehicle, and don't put any music on right away. If the mind winds up its usual jukebox of imagined conversations, notice that. But this time, instead of listening to the sounds of the vehicle, turn on the radio. The radio is better than streaming or a CD player for this exercise because you have no control over what you are about to hear, and you have no expectations. Your ear is a blank canvas.

The first music you hear — it will probably be right in the middle of a phrase, but it doesn't matter — just immediately notice it. If someone is singing, what are the words? Now go further. What instruments are making these sounds? How many instruments would you say there are? Make yourself decide on a number. At this point, is the melody going up or down in pitch? What is the one adjective you would choose to describe the tone of this music? The texture? The tempo? If you could visualize the sound as a structure, what would it look like? What color would it be? If you know the name of the piece or the artist or the year it was written, try not to dwell on that information but rather stick with what is actually happening in the sound. The more specific questions you can answer about the sound, the more the ear will loosen up, and the more it will be able to take in. Say what you hear out loud as you hear it. Deciding on a label helps the mind keep up with the flow of perception.

Eventually, let this conversation you're having with yourself about the sounds fall away and simply take in sound without labeling it. This is virtuoso listening: putting all your attention on the sound, yet doing nothing. If you stop to think, "Wow, I'm getting a lot out of this; I'm listening virtuosically!" you blow it. Just listen, interposing nothing between yourself and the music.

When you make full contact with music like this, no music can ever get old; it is, in the instant, always fresh.

To listen in this way is intensely pleasurable, yet someone sitting next to you might not know it's going on. It's not a particularly emotional experience. When you listen well, you simply perceive the timescape over which all passing emotions play out. All those emotions with which we normally beat ourselves silly pass, while somewhere inside the music we hear time itself flowing silently under them all. Its flowing is the only thing that never changes. To hear it is a great relief.

You can listen to music like this every time you

listen to music. The only reason most people don't is that they forget or don't have the presence of mind to go on a brief fast from compulsive listening. A colleague of mine[6] has an excellent term for the way our ears work in this regard: *earlids*. Because we can see them, we all know we have eyelids. And unless something in our line of sight is truly awful, we rarely choose to close them while we're awake. The default position for our eyelids is open. And yet our earlids, so to speak — those barriers that allow us to ignore musical sound — seem to remain closed by default. It takes very little effort to open them, of course. Anyone can do it at any time. But most people don't. When it comes to the skills required for virtuoso listening, no one is ignorant. Everyone simply ignores.

◆

REMEMBER THAT WHATEVER DESCRIPTION I GIVE OF the listening life will not turn out to be exactly true. Whatever we say it is, it is not that. When you listen well, you go in blind every time, and you find some different truth inside the music every time. That's the whole point. The listening life is always refreshing because it is always being refreshed.

Your listening life can always be expanded. No matter where you are on the spectrum of musical knowledge — occasional listener or master conductor — you can always do more. Everybody is in the same boat here. The skill and attentiveness with which you greet music can always be amplified. Always.

6. Marianne Ploger. See www.plogermethod.com for more on the tricky relationships between the ear, the mind, and real time.

No one catches it all, all the time. Mozart could have done more.

This means there is no arrival point. There is no point in the listening life at which you magically know everything about music, or know all the music there is to know. There is no point at which you may lay down your attention and cruise, no point at which you don't have to try. As a teacher, I see the opposite assumption at work in people all the time; they approach their education as if it all adds up to some summary moment at which they can "get it" and stop trying. It is as if they will one day flip over into a beatific authority because they have put in enough time. They don't notice that this never actually happens in real life. The musicians who appear to be tremendously awake, who speak about and play music with deep authority — and just standing near such a musician is enough to change you — are the people who have realized that music is not magic. It is endless curiosity, endlessly renewed.

The great musicians are the ones who consent to this wiping clean of the ear's slate, this un-knowing that music asks of us, each and every time they play. They agree to hear music's galvanizing lesson about time, which is that there is no such thing as enough of it. They realize there is no way to know what will happen until it happens, and so when we're really listening, every time is heard as the first and last time.

This means the musical ear works like a clear pane of window glass. The window glass is not concerned with storing things up inside itself; it is only interested in disappearing so that light can pass through it unobstructed. In the same way, the ear that is most transparent, the freest from preconception, takes in the most music. An ear that contained everything could perceive nothing. And so music turns our usual ideas about knowledge upside down. In order to grasp whatever it is that music wants to give us, we must always be emptying our hand.

THE REMEMBRANCE OF THINGS PAST

CONSIDER THE SCENE: MILAN, JANUARY 1901. Outside the Grand Hotel on the Via Manzoni, the life of the city passes by almost exactly as usual. Inside the Grand Hotel, a musical legend lies dying. His signature beard, now white, slumps on the humid sheets.[7]

To call Giuseppe Verdi the master of Italian opera is to trivialize him, to place him too neatly on the small throne of historical context. His actual life was big and messy, something like the life of a rock star. Physically abused by his first music teacher, he went on to write music that scandalized the moral establishment and was used as a touchstone anthem for liberal political causes. He had a live-in girlfriend, mountains of money, and a reputation for temper tantrums in rehearsal. His was a remarkable life.

The remarkable thing about the scene of Verdi's death, however, is a subtle thing, easily missed. Here

---

7. A style of beard that still bears his name: the Verdi beard. Most men with beards wear one without realizing it was the composer who first set the trend: moderate length surrounding the jaw line, neatly trimmed.

is a man born in 1813, into a world lit by wax candles, who is dying amid electric light bulbs. Born into a world of letters delivered on horseback, Verdi is dying amid telephones. Born during the career of Napoleon Bonaparte, he is dying during the career of Winston Churchill. Born before the invention of photography, his funeral procession will be captured on silent film. Though the world into which he was born seems unimaginably distant to us, the world in which Verdi dies is, in certain respects, not substantially different from our own. As I write, there are a few people still living who were alive then, too.

Yet at the scene of Verdi's very twentieth-century death, one significant detail carries over from that earlier era into which he was born. One clue tells us a shocking truth about the sound-world in which most of human history has taken place. Outside the Grand Hotel, all over the sidewalks and streets, the citizens of Milan are scattering straw. They are scattering straw in order to dampen the noise of carriages as they pass by Verdi's room.[8]

Imagine for a moment living in a world where the sound of a carriage on cobblestone would be considered offensively loud. Imagine life, even in a populous city, carried out against a backdrop of silence like that. Now imagine listening to music in such silence. In that quietness, how vivid would the mere presence of musical sound be? It would be impossible not to pay attention to music.

Is it simply because our machinery has gotten louder

8. See Charles Osborne, *Verdi: A Life in the Theatre* (London: Weidenfeld and Nicolson, 1987) 326. My thanks to Carl Smith for first pointing out this significant detail to me.

that we sometimes fail to notice music? Perhaps, but I believe the principal reason is something much more insidious than that, insidious because it comes to us disguised as music itself. As the storybook coincidence of history would have it, that distraction is being born in Milan in January 1901, less than a mile, in fact, from where Verdi lies dying.

At 6 Via Dante, in the studios of the Anglo-Italian Commerce Company, a portly young tenor is laying down wax cylinder recordings.[9] He is, incidentally, recording some of Verdi's music. But making recordings like this is a cumbersome task. Once engraved, the wax cylinders cannot be duplicated, so the tenor must repeat his performance for each and every recording produced. To buy one of these recordings is to buy a one-of-a-kind rendition, and to play it is to erase it. Each delicate cylinder can be played only a limited number of times before its wax impression wears out, leaving behind only a garbled hiss.

Of course, sound recording had been around for a long time; Thomas Edison had invented the phonograph over twenty years earlier in 1877. His invention sat largely ignored, however, for the first ten years of its life, and — strangely, to our way of thinking — the idea of using it to record music had never really caught on. No one wanted to bother with the impractical wax cylinders, and perhaps to the nineteenth-century mind it was simply unnecessary. Why listen to the poor-mouthed imitation of music when you could just listen to music?

9. See Roland Gelatt, *The Fabulous Phonograph*, 2nd revised ed. (New York: Macmillan, 1977) 104.

And yet our young tenor presses on, giving his all for each new cylinder. His is a forceful personality. His name is Enrico Caruso, and within three unbelievably short years — thanks to the invention of the reproducible shellac disc — he will become the first person ever to sell one million records.

In Milan, January 1901, just a few city blocks separate all that music was from all it would become. Here at the turn of the twentieth century, music is leaving the immeasurable silence in which it had always existed and is becoming a constantly available thing. Music is leaving the realm of real time — in which it can possess us — and entering the realm of the recorded object — through which we can possess it. Music is becoming, in a word, smaller.

♦

NOW I WOULD LIKE TO STRESS THAT I AM IN NO WAY suggesting a return to times past, as if the key to fulfilling listening could be found in the pre-recorded era simply because people had nothing better to do. I would just like to point out that for most of us, there is practically no difference between the idea of music and the idea of recordings. We experience most of our music via recordings of some kind. If we examine our everyday experience, we realize that, by-and-large, music is the recording, and the recording is music. In our minds, the two experiences are not separate.

Even when we go to a live performance, there is the ever-present comparison of that performance with the sound of a recorded version remembered in our heads. Or if the live music is new to us, we know we can get a recording of it afterwards. (The root of the word "record" is from the Latin word for "to remember." In other words, we assume all music can be remembered for us by recordings.) We know this even as we listen, and so we listen with divided attention. The existence of recording trammels even our live listening experience; the recording stands between us and the sound. We are not all the way there because we don't have to be.

Many of us never stop to imagine what listening to music would be like without the possibility of recording. The music begins and . . . *here it comes, this is it, this is the only time you will ever, ever, ever hear this . . . are you catching it?* It will never be exactly the same, even if the same performers repeat it. To imagine listening with such rapacious attention is to see that the mere existence of recording technology dilutes the experience of music. Recordings keep us from that experience by sheltering us from the necessity of total listening.

Of course, on a practical level, I am not at all suggesting that we avoid recordings. Many of us became lovers of music because a recording first hooked our attention. But we should at least notice that music itself — in its pure form as an experience — stands quite apart from recording. In fact, recordings do violence to music by tampering with its time-flow, its most essential fabric. Recordings can be reversed, fast-forwarded, and paused. Through recordings, we can do all the things to music that we would love to be able do to our own lives, but never can. We can dam up and re-route the flow of time in which music exists. We can dissect the living creature.

We might even say that recordings allow us to remove music from time. Recordings can be repeated exactly, while the unique instants of life never can, though we have all felt the awkward disappointment of trying. Recordings offer an escape from the stark, completely final passage of time that music, when we listen fully, shows us. Recordings tell us a poisonously soft lie about time, while music tells us the truth.

You have felt this in your own experience. The first time you hear a great piece of music on a recording, that first hearing is the truth. It is what we might call the "holy shit moment." Here is the shit of everyday life — doing this chore, forgetting to do that one — and suddenly it is made holy. Suddenly you see, inside the sounding of that music, that everything you are doing is, in some obscure way, real, that it all counts, that it all matters, every last instant the clock erases forever. You have received, you have felt in your gut, the lesson of all music. If in this moment you smashed the recording to bits, there would be no problem.

The problem comes weeks later when you have played and re-played the recording until the experience starts to sour. You get a little sick of the music. A slight nausea, a restlessness arises because you have been fooled. You thought that the wild charge you felt on the first hearing resided inside the music. It never did. That music, if it was well-crafted, simply tripped you over into the true perception of time, the ruthless *now* of your own life. But by taking an exact repetition of that music and sounding it over and over, you actually destroy this perception of time. You pretend that a section of your life can be repeated. You endeavor to preserve a section of your own time. That endeavor, as music teaches us, is always a failure.

So there is a difference between the heightened experience of ourselves we call music and this game of pretend that recordings let us play. Through recordings, we can insulate ourselves in a cocoon of exactly what we want to hear. But music is here to pull us out of that cocoon and into the knotty, refreshing reality of sound beyond our narrow tastes and weak desires. If we never notice recordings for what they are, we run the risk of experiencing only our own experience of music, and never music itself.

To see the use of recordings as completely distinct from the experience of music is not difficult when we consider what a recent development recording is. Music was being made and listened to eons before written language, agriculture, or the development of cities. It is far older than the practice of remembering or recording our own existence, even in words. Whatever experience was there in human history, music was there concurrent with it, simultaneous with it, amplifying the listener's sense of presence in that present instant, improvised and then gone forever. By contrast, the ability to divide time by freezing snippets of it in recording has been around for barely one hundred years, a proverbial eye-blink in the span of human development. Think of it this way: almost everyone reading this book has parents or grandparents whose lives overlapped with that of Thomas Edison.[10]

The advantages of recording are so great that we don't notice the subtle pleasure we gave up in gaining them. Consider, for example, the Edison Gramophone Company's "Tone Tests," conducted as

---

10. Edison died in 1931.

part of an advertising campaign in the late 1910s. These exhibitions took place in concert halls before a live audience. The stage was set with an Edison gramophone. A professional singer began the show by walking out, starting the machine, and singing along a cappella with a recording of her own voice. The point of the exhibition was that she could dupe the audience by randomly stopping, starting, and dovetailing the live and recorded voices, illustrating the supposedly indistinguishable closeness of the two.[11]

For the final number, with dramatic panache, the theater was completely darkened. The singer began alone and then, under cover of dark, started the gramophone, stopped her live performance, and left the stage unnoticed, leaving the audience to disbelieve their eyes when the lights were turned up, revealing the gramophone alone on stage. According to contemporary accounts, none of the audience of the day could distinguish between the live voice and the recorded one.[12]

Of course, these accounts were published by the Edison Company, and so to say that no one circa 1917 could tell the difference between the live and the recorded music is probably an exaggeration of advertising. Moreover, the singers were practiced at singing along impeccably with their own recordings. So let's be cautious and say it was true that half the audience could not tell the difference. The implications are still bewildering.

---

11. See Emily Thompson, "Machines, Music, and the Quest for Fidelity," in *The Musical Quarterly*, vol. 79, no. 1 (Spring 1995), pp. 131–33.

12. See Thompson, 157–58.

Imagine the sound of a 78-rpm record. Even assuming the record is in mint condition, imagine it being played through a hand-cranked gramophone. Now imagine that gramophone, with its single metal horn serving as a speaker, at a distance of thirty or forty feet. Contrast that sound in your imagination with the sound of a classically trained soprano, live, singing with her whole body, animating the air all around you with full vowels, hard consonants, overtones, vibrato — an actual human voice. If you were in the same room, is there really any chance you would not be able to tell the two apart?

Here, of course, we enter the realm of pure speculation, but it's as if Edison's audience was listening to something else entirely. When they heard a recording — the fidelity of which would almost certainly drive us to distraction — they did not notice the recording *qua* recording because they were simply listening to music, to the fact that music was sounding. The recording, for them, was not yet an object, a thing that can be looked at as separate from the experience of music in time. For their ears, the "main event" was the bare presence of music, be it live or recorded.

The innocence of such an ear, the ability to take music as a happening in time and nothing more, is lost when the technology of recording itself becomes a fetish. Between their time and ours stands a constantly widening separation of recording as commercial object from the experience of listening itself. Now we can, ironically, use recordings to drown out the language of time that music speaks. Skipping from one track to the next within narrow style categories, we miss out on the destructive aspect of listening, the power of music to obliterate our private tastes in an ocean of sonic fact.

◆

WHEN WE DIP INTO THE REALITY OF MUSIC THROUGH true listening and see that music itself is not a thing located in our recordings, we have to ask: where was music located, so to speak, in the pre-recorded era? Unless the music was sounding out loud, it was locked inside the score or inside the mind of the performer. For musicians who did not read music but simply improvised around remembered tunes or invented them on the spot, we can only imagine what that music felt like in a mind uninformed by recordings, i.e. a mind for which exact repetition was impossible. How present they must have been in the act of performance, how unhindered by reflection and comparison.

In the case of literate musicians, the situation was even farther from our own. Unlike reading musicians today, who may almost always listen to a recording as they learn from the printed score, musicians throughout most of the last millennium had to lift the piece directly off the page with no help. This resulted in a different kind of literacy, a more direct connection between eye and ear. It was, to use a common phrase, the ability to "hear with the eyes and see with the ears";[13] that is, the ability to read a musical score while sitting in silence, hearing the music just as you "hear" the words of this book internally as you read. While such clarity of imagination has always

13. Probably a misquotation of Robert Schumann. See "Aphorisms" in *On Music and Musicians* (New York: Pantheon, 1946) 30–51.

been rare in its fully developed form, there is no reason to doubt that it was more developed — along with the ability to play scores at the piano — in the pre-recorded era. On most days, unless you could afford a group of performers or admission to a concert, such interaction with scores was the only alternative to silence.

Skillful interaction with the printed score may have reached its zenith with the Hungarian pianist and composer Franz Liszt. An American composer named Otis Boise, who visited Liszt in Germany in the 1870s, told the story of bringing Liszt the full orchestral score of one of his own compositions for Liszt to critique. Boise handed Liszt the score. (Bear in mind that an orchestral score generally contains fifteen-plus staves of music, in different clefs, sounding simultaneously). Liszt looked it over in silence, laid it down, then walked over to his piano and played the entire thing from memory, with running commentary.[14]

Such ferocious capability for musical intake was matched by the Russian composer Sergei Rachmaninoff. When Rachmaninoff was a student at the Moscow Conservatory in the 1880s, a friend named Alchevsky played for him at the piano the first movement of a symphony in progress. Three years later, Rachmaninoff met Alchevsky again and asked how his symphony was coming along. Alchevsky admitted that he had finished the first movement and then given up. Rachmaninoff replied that this was a shame because he enjoyed very much the movement he had heard, one time only, three

---

14. See Harold C. Schonberg, *The Great Pianists* (New York: Simon and Schuster, 1963) 165–66.

years before. He then went to the piano and played it back for Alchevsky in its entirety.[15]

Of course, these are exceptional cases, and certainly examples of prodigious musical literacy occur after the advent of recorded sound as well. But this kind of live-wire connection between score, sound, and memory is something recording has caused most of us to stop working towards entirely. We hear these stories and write them off as the quirks of a savant, or we turn to brain science to try and explain them away. The kind of attention that Liszt and Rachmaninoff must have been paying, however, is the *sine qua non* of their staggering feats. And anyone can pay any amount of attention at any time, though our saturation with recordings has convinced us that we don't have to do so. We can always play it again, and so we never quite catch all the music the first time around. We are always listening casually. At every moment, music has the power to change us, but we are always holding that power at arm's length.

---

15. See Victor Seroff, *Rachmaninoff* (New York: Simon and Schuster, 1950) 40.

Heavy Marble Gods

W**E HAVE JUST MENTIONED SOME OF THE** "heroes" of classical music. We have looked into the past as a way of framing our own assumptions about listening. But if we are serious about music's power to change the way we think of time, we must acknowledge a danger that lurks behind this captivating story of classical music. This chapter is, to some extent, shop talk among classical musicians, but it is also a *mea culpa* on behalf of us all.

Let's face it: when I write a book about music while looking out from the classical music establishment, the expectation is that I will be looking down. Classical music, in the minds of most people, is actually defined by a certain sense of superiority. In defense of this superiority, the clichés pile up: this is "the greatest music ever written" that has "withstood the test of time"; these are performers who have "spent their whole lives" learning to play music that is "profoundly enriching"; and so on. The expectation is that I will continue telling this story of superiority.

Instead, I am going to tell the truth. To hear the

truth, we must distinguish between the living tradition of music itself and the dead cultural barnacle that is generally called "classical music" today. Classical music in this latter sense trusses up the idea of oldness to achieve its perceived superiority. It actively tries to avoid the present moment in which the listener lives; it offers an escape. If we define music as an art that draws us more fully into the current of time, then this inflated posturing about the value of old music is actually the opposite of music.

But the predilection for a sense of oldness in classical music is more than just a marketing ploy. It is grounded in a sincere reverence for great music that happens to have been written in the past. And a fixed canon of this music, unfortunately, pushes everything else out; most symphony and opera programs contain no music by living composers. And so, no matter how flawless the performance, no matter how luxurious the hall, there is always a disturbing flavor about the whole affair, a sense that the real thing — the momentous event of great music — is over.

In other words, classical music's fetish for the idea of the past is at least honest. People (myself included) sincerely love the canon of Western art music — the "three Bs" (Bach, Beethoven, and Brahms), as it were. Yet our love disturbs us. And classical music remains uninteresting and irrelevant to the majority of listeners because it offers almost no music written during their lifetime. The whole situation is absurd, but we don't see it because we work inside its boundaries. We should realize that this situation has never before occurred in the history of music, and in no other genre of music would it be tolerated. The whole point of listening to music in other genres is to hear something new, something that says something about *now*.

When we, as purveyors and lovers of classical music look back and wonder where the golden age went, when we feel nostalgia for the era of our own relevance, we fail to notice an obvious distinction between our time and the time in which the canon was born. In the heyday of classical music, there was no such thing as "classical music." In other words, there was no such thing as music set apart and protected for its supposed greatness as distinct from new music. Today, "new music" in the classical profession is a tiny subset of the whole art, one that barely makes an appearance on mainstream concerts except as the dreaded oddity snuck in before the concerto. Classical players are trained to think that playing music written by living persons is a rarified specialty. But in the golden age of classical music, this situation — i.e., to our minds, classical music — didn't exist. All music was new music. Conversely, the death of new music has been the death of classical music, save for its existence as a subsidized shell of vague cultural fanciness and a shaky employer of music majors.

If you have ever studied the history of classical music, you know that this bizarre separation of working composers and the listening public occurred gradually during the first half of the twentieth century. The usual explanation, in a nutshell, is that composers during this period started writing ugly music — music without a tonal center, without a memorable tune, without a regular beat. But it is also worth noticing that as these twentieth-century composers reflected with honesty the realities of their world — mechanized warfare, genocide, and the threat of nuclear annihilation — the listening public averted their ears and escaped into early classical music, which had just been made readily available on recording. Suddenly, thanks to recordings, the classical music public had an alternative to reality. They had a fixed canon of great music, vaulted off from the age in which they lived.

And so it follows that the current audience has no taste for new music because they expect new music to match up with the great yardstick of that recorded and re-recorded canon. Armed with fifteen different recordings of the Beethoven symphonies, they are disappointed when the one ten-minute piece of music by a living composer that they actually hear in a year isn't as good. Of course, it isn't as good; what are the statistical chances it would be as good? Such a listener forgets that Beethoven's audience was willing to sit through a hundred lesser symphonies by now-forgotten composers in order to get one Beethoven symphony. Beethoven's audience paid their dues in a way that today's audience will not because today's audience has the recording industry to filter everything else out for them. Beethoven's listeners had no music except the music being played in the room they were in. They had, as it were, a very short musical memory. And so, as a paying audience, they supported the long, hard battle to articulate in sound what it is the present moment means. In other words, they supported the production of masterpieces. Today's audience throws the word "masterpiece" around like a magical incantation, but refuses to do the listening work required to produce one. This makes the hearing of the Beethoven symphony not a pleasurable memory of a past masterpiece but a desperate clinging to "inspiration," "genius," and other baldly superstitious concepts.

Today, the sense of history inherent in recordings gives the music of previous centuries a concrete reality it never had before. Suddenly, composers have to make it onto recordings to enter the canon, and so the canon acquires a solidity and a sense of importance that freezes us with anxiety. Recordings have made our memory so heavy that our memory has crushed us. We look back at the history of classical music and see a captivating story. But the heroes of that story, when they were actually writing their great music, were not consciously participating in any story. They were simply working. When we look back at their work and call it a story, we can no longer see ourselves as part of it. We no longer have the courage to believe in the reality of our own time, to believe that the big questions can still be answered in sound by us. We forget that compared to the ancient art of music, the lifespan of the classical canon is as that of a housefly.

This affected humility in the face of the canon results, ironically, in the grossest kind of self-importance on the part of classical musicians. When our art form devolves into the same repertoire being played over and over and over by different performers — a kind of macho contest to see who tackles the same old warhorse best — then the art form is obviously about those performers, not about the repertoire. The performers are simply riding the canon's perceived importance as a vehicle for their own careers.

Our establishment compensates for this brazen

careerism with the fable of old music's wholesomeness. We play and listen to music as if the music itself — specifically, eighteenth- and nineteenth-century German music — contains some magical vitamin that will instantly bless us with culture, depth, and class. We treat music as a possession that we can accrue and use to feel better about ourselves. It is a way to impress our friends, a less expensive version of collecting antique brandy. This attitude is a kind of incense that we classical musicians will gladly use to mask our own rotting irrelevance. Thankfully, most of the listening public can smell right through it.

Let me be clear once again: I love the canon, I adore it. Learning it changed me. I think it is one of the pinnacle achievements in human history, and I incessantly nag my students to get to know more of it. There is no debating classical music's value; it is indeed unspeakably valuable. The problem is that it is considered valuable for the wrong reasons. To treat our classical music as if it contained some secret greatness down inside itself because it has "withstood the test of time" is to miss the point of music altogether. Such an approach to listening actually fails the test of time. Music is here to show us our own tremendous responsibility toward the age in which we live by altering the way we listen to time pass. That transformation takes place inside us — not inside the great music. To act as if it does is to shirk our own responsibility.

No piece of music, no matter how great, will save us. Listening to Beethoven's Ninth can change your life, but listening to a dog bark can change your life too. Great music simply makes it easier. In the face of great music, we are sometimes forced into total listening, into a better kind of contact with the world around us. Rather than misuse great music as an escape into a fantasy of times past, we must use it to ask ourselves a simple question: at every moment, am I listening to what is happening right now? Am I listening to the only moment in which I am alive? If any music stands in the way of that listening, it would be better for such music to be burned, erased, and forgotten.

◆

TO SAY THAT MUSIC EXPRESSES SOMETHING ABOUT the present moment is not, however, just a matter of the listener's experience. Everyone knows that the way time seems to pass during a piece of music is also one of the best ways we have of describing that music's style. Often, it is problematic to point to certain harmonies or rhythms in a piece and say that this is a composer's style. Style is more slippery than that; style is an attempt to describe how those concrete materials are used or what the space between them is like. Articulating how a composer divides time with musical objects is a better way of discovering his or her style than simply describing those objects. The way a piece of music handles time tells us something, in turn, about the time in which that music was written. Music is a kind of fossil imprint of how time feels at a given point in history.

To illustrate, allow me to use three well known composers: Mozart (1756–1791), Brahms (1833–1897), and Philip Glass (born in 1937, still very much alive and working as I write). If you don't know some music by these composers, try finding a brief sample of each online before you continue reading. A few minutes of each will make it easy to hear what I'm talking about.

As you listen to music by Mozart, you can hear how time flows along at a regular pace. (We are not talking about tempo here, but rather the subjective sense of time's progression as we listen.) If you wanted to put your finger on Mozart's style, you might say that with Mozart, time is divided in a rational way. This is music of the high Enlightenment, after all, and events of similar proportion follow one another with no break in a more-or-less predictable way. Time in Mozart's world sounds like clockwork, a regular and well-regulated thing.

Now compare that with the music of Brahms, writing one hundred years later, using many of the exact same chords and formal structures. The timescape with Brahms is much more dicey. In this later music, the flow of time can suddenly be dammed up or catch in an eddy. We can feel ourselves floating over a sustained harmony. We can feel the cool breath of doubt seeping in through the slight disproportions in the way a Romantic-era composer parses time. One line of counterpoint can even seem to move at a pace somehow different from the others.

Move ahead another one hundred years to Philip Glass. Here the flow of time can start out stopped; from a perfectly still center, it can delight us by spiraling outward, backward, sideways, forward, or not at all. The timescape is no longer a line along which we must travel, but a space through which we can move.

Mozart, Brahms, and Glass — three radically different composers from three radically different centuries. And yet if you look at their scores you will find, on a local level, many of the exact same materials: major and minor triads, evenly pulsing rhythms, and formal structures predicated on repetition. The difference between these composers is best described as a matter of time, understood as the field between, behind, and around the objective events on which analysis has traditionally focused. How are the musical objects arranged, and what assumptions about time does the arrangement belie?

To speak about this background field of time in a composer's world is necessarily a subjective act. Like quantum mechanics, it involves the perceiving subject as an inseparable part of the object being measured. But nothing prevents us from being "objective" in the colloquial sense — that is to say, clear-headed — about the nature of our subjective listening experiences. To be honest about style, we must observe ourselves — the listening subject — as object too.

Thinking about musical style as time-play shows us the danger in worshiping music of the past. When we feel those different assumptions about time that music can hold, it changes the way we listen to the music of earlier centuries. Let's use the same three composers, Mozart, Brahms, and Glass, as examples. In a certain sense, we can no longer listen honestly to a sonata form by Mozart or Brahms because that form no longer speaks to the way we experience time in our daily lives. For us, the music of Glass represents the only sincere music, the only music that answers honestly the non-linear nature of a world in which instantaneous communication is always possible. We cannot really hear the sonata form by Mozart or Brahms sincerely because, for instance, we no longer have to write a letter and then wait days, weeks, or months for the reply like a recapitulation. We cannot ache for a tonal cadence in the same manner because the narrative trip forward in time is not a necessity for us. It can be a nostalgic fantasy perhaps, but not a necessity. We know that we can always jump to the reply; similarly, the tonic harmony is already here, and in truth it never left. Our technology has nearly eradicated desire, and so to listen to music in which that desire forward in time is an unquestioned assumption is to indulge in a kind of escapism.

I am not here to argue for or against the era in which we live, only to point out that we live in it, and that the music being written in it is the only music we can hear and perform completely honestly. Realizing this actually makes listening to the music of previous eras more, not less, exciting. Not only do we get to hear great music, we also get to experience the bizarre assumptions that earlier civilizations had about time. And it may well be that those assumptions challenge our own and help us perceive aspects of time that our own era ignores. (As when, for example, in the 1970s, Arvo Pärt broke free from lockstep modernism and arrived at his spacious minimalism through a study of medieval chant.) We hear the different stories people have told about time, and we gain perspective on what time really is, beyond all those stories. Individual pieces of music, however, can never be fully separated from the age in which they were written.

So when we listen to the music of previous centuries, we must do so mindfully, recognizing that we can never completely participate in that music's worldview. The canon as we know it is great music. But it is music that can never, ever speak for us. To treat the music of the past as a talisman and reverence it exclusively makes us not just irrelevant to our listening public, but out-and-out delusional about the nature of our own existence.

◆

HOWEVER MUCH WE WOULD LIKE TO SAY THAT there is a finite amount of important classical music and that we know all of it, a friction exists between the idea of a fixed musical canon and music itself. For music, like time, will never stop blasting to bits the fictions of older generations. We can't imagine it, but if the globe turns long enough, Bach, Beethoven, and Brahms will all be forgotten. It is only a matter of enough time. What is it about music that stands outside of time? For if music belongs to time — if it is a thing, an object, a tradition that we can learn and then drag kicking and screaming out of the past and into the future — then it is destined to die. In order to sustain itself, it must destroy itself. If music as an art form is to live on, individual pieces of music must constantly be forgotten.

This paradox was shown to us most clearly by a piece that premiered just as commercial recordings were setting the story of the familiar classical canon firmly in stone. The year was 1953, and the piece was John Cage's *4'33"*.[16] As anyone who has studied music knows, *4'33"* famously consists of pure silence — four minutes and thirty-three seconds of it, to be exact. You might say it

---

16. See Kyle Gann, *No Such Thing as Silence: John Cage's 4'33"* (New Haven: Yale University Press, 2010).

is a piece of anti-music. It is composed of no sounds whatsoever.

More precisely, *4'33"* is composed of whatever sounds happen in the concert space. Listening to the piece is an exercise in accepting the unadorned sound of that duration. What does four minutes and thirty-three seconds of your life actually sound like?

Any performance of *4'33"* I've ever been a part of has followed a similar dramatic curve, a regular shape to how the silence behaves. The first minute is always the quietest, because many of the audience believe the performer is just centering himself before beginning to play. Then, around minute two, there's often a wave of sound from the audience: "Oh, I get it," chuckles, and some remarks of annoyance. Then, the magic of the piece takes place. In the latter half of the allotted time, everyone (performers included) can go one of two ways: either they get lost in the voices inside their head — replaying old conversations and making future plans — or they accept what is actually happening and participate in the silence around them. Those who acknowledge the fact of the silence and face it head-on find that their ears wake up to sounds they weren't noticing when they sat down. What was a forced silence at the beginning of the piece becomes a living silence by the end, pulsing with raw sensitivity. When *4'33"* is over, if a single note were to be played, it would be an event, and no one would miss it. Thanks to Cage's non-music, we arrive at the state in which all music should be heard. We become "all ears."

Incidentally, Cage also wrote a piece called *Organ2/ ASLAP*, which stands for "as slow and long as possible." Currently, a performerless church organ in Halberstadt,

Germany, is playing the piece using weights on the keys that are changed every few years. Though the performance began in 2001, it hasn't yet gotten through the first page of score. If everything stays in tempo, the piece will end in the year 2640, a total duration of 639 years.

Perhaps no other composer has ever written two more different pieces. From the same man we have less than five minutes of silence and 639 years of sound. Yet both pieces point to the same truth about music: it is measured time, nothing more. The ruthlessness of the measurement is hammed up in Cage, but it is present in all music. This measurement will never allow us to be passive observers, and it will never allow us to remove ourselves from the story of the great repertoire, for as soon as music hits our ears, we are the thing being measured.

III. TRANSFORMATION

LIVING IN TEMPO

S O FAR, WE HAVE SEEN THIS MUCH: COMPLETE
absorption in music occasionally trips us into a
state of mind that might be called non-reflective.[17] In the
non-reflective state, we have no thoughts about what we
are doing; we are simply doing it. We are not having a
response to a thing while it is still going on. In fact, even
to say that we are in the non-reflective state is to throw
ourselves out of it. When we are in it, all our attention is
burned up by sheer experience, and there is no room for
self-consciousness. And if there is no self-consciousness,
then there is no room for awkwardness, fear, or pain
to take hold. The non-reflective state is, in fact, quite
pleasurable.

Yet we live in a highly reflective age. Our first tendency
is not to be consumed by experience, but to reflect on
it and try to preserve it as it is happening. We reserve
part of ourselves and spend part of our energy trying to
capture the experience midstream. We even label our

---

17. I am borrowing the term (as opposed to simply
"unreflective") from Thomas Keating. See *Open Mind, Open Heart*
(New York: Continuum, 2002) 74.

own emotions as they occur. In other words, we react to our reactions to experience. (Perhaps you have noticed that hardly anyone cries anymore; rather they stop to say, "This is making me cry!" Nor do most people really get lost in laughter; they only stop to say, "That's funny!")

Through reflection, we set up a conceptual image of our experience, an image that stands between us and the real thing. We walk around with a scrim of thought between ourselves and the world. The reflective state is draining and anxiety-ridden, because this scrim of thought always scrambles the truth. There is the truth of what is happening around us, and then there is our personal reflection on it, which is never exactly true. Most days, we touch only the dim, half-true reflection, and never life itself.

We write about events as they happen, we stop to post a picture, we comment and opine in real time — or perhaps I should say in false time, because no one who is trying to capture reality can be all the way present with reality — as if we were trying to affix a marker to our experience so that later we can return to it.

When we attempt to return, we are always disappointed by what we find. Real life — in real time — allows for no reflection. It is all uncaptureable. Our tendency to reflect is an expression of anxiety over this fact.

And so the question arises: if we spend most of our time trafficking in unreal reflections of life, and if music offers us the chance to drop these reflections and live in real time, can music improve the way we live? Is it possible to have a more musical life? Obviously, just playing music in the background may not help us very much. But the starkly true perspective into which music occasionally trips us — what would it look like to go there voluntarily?

We have already seen what this non-reflective state looks like in the listener. But anyone who has ever performed music onstage knows the difference between the reflective and the non-reflective state quite intimately. Keeping the two separate is a skill that takes most performing musicians years to cultivate.

Picture this: you are backstage before your concert, you can hear the noise of the crowd settling in, and the people backstage are trying to make conversation with you. Meanwhile, the instrument in your hands, which you have played for years, suddenly feels like a foreign object. The blood is drained from your hands, and the music you are about to walk out and play, well . . . you can't double-check it anymore. Will it still be there, in the mind's eye, in the memory? The question makes you feel dizzy, as if the floor were shifting beneath your feet. So you run through the first couple of bars quietly again and again.

But now the crowd and the people backstage are silent. They have betrayed you. The performance has come, and suddenly you are walking out on stage without having really decided to do so. You are simply being carried along by the evening, riding the clock-hand into what seems like an absurd gamble.

So, sidestepping your own nerves, you begin. And, of course, the music is all right there. Playing from memory, you do not have to remember the whole hour of music; you only have to remember the phrase at hand. It is easy. It goes well. It is fun.

And then, something goes ever-so-slightly wrong — maybe a wrong note, or maybe not even something as noticeable as that — maybe a wrong fingering or a shaky rhythm — a mistake that ninety-nine percent of the audience doesn't even notice. It goes by and is completely forgotten. Forgotten, that is, by everyone except you.

By now you are several bars on from the mistake, and all your focus ought to be on playing *this* phrase, *this* note convincingly. But instead, you are replaying the bungle in your mind. You are in the reflective state, and suddenly a dangerous gap opens up between what you are thinking about and what you are actually doing. You are distracted (the Latin root of which literally means "pulled apart"). In other words, you are pulled away from the task at hand and backwards in time. In your mind, you are listening to music that has already happened.

Or perhaps you are playing an easy passage, but you are dreading the difficult passage to come. In an attempt to get prepared for the difficult passage, you let your mind pull you far out ahead of where you are in the music. Again, the mind has separated itself from the hands and is attempting to be in a moment that doesn't yet exist.

As all performers know, it is in this distraction — this gap opened up when you are pulled backwards or forwards in time — that the really nightmarish mistakes happen. In both cases, there is a paradox at work: the fastest way to make yourself look bad is to think about how you look. And in both cases, the illusion is that you can be anywhere other than where you are in time. The best frame of mind for a performer is to ignore this false possibility until the mind rights itself in a state of presence. The word *presence* is sometimes overused to refer to a vague sense of someone's personality or charisma, but here I simply mean *presence* as in *the present*, not the past or the future — not even by a beat — but this present note, this present sound. There is nothing vague about presence in this sense. Your attention is either undivided or divided, wholly inside this moment or pulled apart.

The great, non-reflective performer is so completely with the present note that everything she plays seems easy — easy because within the frame of the present there is only ever this note, and a single note is never difficult. It sounds simple to do, but the tendency to want to go back and fix something or look ahead and prepare (both of which are secretly impossible) is so ingrained that most of us waste tremendous amounts of energy dancing on either side of presence to the sound. Of course, the option is always open to us. But we prefer to squirm.[18]

Overcoming this habitual squirm and performing from a state of presence teaches us a funny thing about time past. After you observe enough notes going by — the brilliant ones and the flubs alike — you realize that there really is no going back. What's over is completely unrepeatable; each tiny second, as it passes, can never be reached again. And so practically, there is no difference between a note that sounded five seconds ago and the building of the Giza pyramids. Both events are equally vanished. If neither can be gone back to, then in practical terms one is not any "closer" than the other.

The point of view of the non-reflective performer, then, is one that is completely unburdened. It is

---

18. See Barry Green, *The Inner Game of Music* (New York: Doubleday, 1986) for a further discussion of inner self-distraction onstage.

unburdened because it is free from the weight of time. In music, time cannot accrue like money in an account. Once it is past, it has no real existence. And this view of time, which we find at the highest levels of musical performance, can be adopted by anyone. You know it by its feeling of tremendous freedom. In this instant, this note, this string, this interval, there is never any problem. Here — just here — there is nothing but empty structure and the clearness of fact. To see it is not absorption; it is actually freedom from our usual absorption in past and future events. To enjoy this state of freedom, we have to relinquish our usual belief that we can be anywhere other than where we are.

◆

THE GREAT THING ABOUT THIS MUSICAL, OR NON-reflective sense of time is that you can immediately tell whether someone is in it or not. We all have a sixth sense as to whether someone else is present or absent in conversation. You can see it behind the eyes quite clearly. It is almost as if you can see the screen of thought that prevents people from noticing what is happening in front of them. Of course, noticing it in others is easier. We are much less likely to notice when we ourselves are lost in reflection.

The trick to cutting through this veil of distraction is attention, and by that I mean a constantly cultivated habit of attention, not just the kind we automatically pay whenever something beautiful or terrifying slaps us into it. And yet, to say "pay attention" only does so much good. Effort alone has nothing to do with it.

My job at the university is to teach the subject

traditionally called "ear training." I teach musicians how to hear certain chords, scales, rhythms, and so on, and how to sing them at sight and write them down by ear. And, of course, like any teacher, I often find myself saying, "Pay attention to this!" Ostensibly, I am saying "pay attention to this kind of harmony," or "pay attention to this scale degree," and so on. But unless a person is paying attention to the fact that there is music sounding at all, asking for such discernment does no good. And I find that many people are not, in fact, paying attention to what is happening in the room right now. People are usually paying attention to their thoughts about what is happening in the room, or else to their thoughts about something else entirely.

It happens to us all. When that mental barrier gets dropped between us and the actual events around us, we project images of past and future onto it, and we do not really see where we are. We are not giving our attention out; we are mistakenly trying to conserve attention, trying to pull it in and save it. But the tricky paradox of attention is this: you only possess as much attention as you give away.

We can especially notice this preference for mental images of life over life itself when we are surrounded by something beautiful. Last winter, for instance, I was taking a walk in the river bottoms that surround our neighborhood. The woods were covered in snow, the trail was empty, and as I crossed a footbridge, I was so struck by the symmetry of the scene — the white ribbon of trail bending into the forest, still unmarked by my crunching shoes — that I stopped to take a picture.

I then walked on across the bridge and, eventually,

through an open field. The field was even more beautiful than the bridge, the grays and whites of the landscape now flecked with blue jays, cardinals, and deep spruce. Yet walking through that scene, I almost missed it entirely because as I walked across the field, I was thinking about the picture I had taken back at the bridge. I was talking to myself about how I would frame the picture and where in the house I would hang it. The brilliance of the field only barely cut through my woolgathering about the already-taken photograph and visions of plastic picture frames from the drugstore. I had to laugh at myself. My legs were moving and my mind was running, but I was completely absent.

We can also notice our tendency to reflect in interactions with other people. Often, when we look at another person, we do not see that person but rather a series of remembered images from past meetings. We see, projected on the wall of thought behind our eyes, pictures of their past behavior. Perhaps they were cruel to us, rejected us, or embarrassed us in some way. We are angered by these images, and so we become agitated, even though at this moment the person in front of us is doing nothing. Or perhaps in the past they behaved with such amazing goodness or skill that we feel awed by our image of the person, and so we are unable to speak clearly to them in the moment.

It doesn't matter if the past images are painful or pleasant; in both cases, the remembrance of them causes feelings to arise that distract us from who the person really is. Hatred and hero-worship have exactly the same effect. We become awkward and mannered. We cannot look the other person in the eye for very long, and we don't exactly know what to do with our feet. We spend most days like this — talking to phantoms, to creations of our own imagination, rather than to real people. It is exhausting work.

The alternative, of course, is to place all our attention on what is in the room at this precise moment. And what is here in the room? A person — two eyes, into which you are always free to look — a body, maybe some words they are choosing to speak, which in turn stand for events floating around in their mind — nothing else. If you place all your attention outward in this way, you see that there is almost never a problem in this room. Unless the person is trying to attack you physically, there is no need to react. There is no need for the fidgeting, anxiety, and aimless thinking that your images from the past conjure up in you. You can always deal with whatever is happening right now. To realize that events in the past literally do not exist, that they are simply bundles of neurons twitching in your brain and yours alone, is to regain tremendous amounts of energy. The crucial skill is to be able to tell the difference between an emotional hangover from past interactions and what is actually happening. Ask yourself in every moment: is there a problem in this room?

When you answer that question truthfully, you regain the composure most adults have thrown away. You can look another person in the eye without fear, and you can see what needs to be done. You can do it, and then forget about it. You feel lighter somehow, and your work becomes more effective. You realize that action always feels better than thought. You learn to take accurate action, the kind based on present conditions, as opposed to imaginary past-and-future conditions. You see that action can always happen, but that it can only ever happen where you are. You learn to live in tempo.

The freshness that comes from living in tempo is something for which everyone is constantly searching. Life feels stale, and, as one songwriter puts it, we all want to go back to a time " . . . when the sky was more blue / and the whole thing was new."[19] So few people find this sense of freshness because they think they can either remember their way back to it or somehow arrange things so it will come again in the future. They don't notice that their private fantasy of past and future is precisely the thing that blocks their view of the freshness.

It is as if you were in a house, trying to look out a window with a movie screen hung in front of it. You want to look out the window and see the sun, but you keep getting sucked into the story of the characters projected onto the screen. Over and over again, you sit indoors in the dark and watch the same movies — inanimate, flat images of things. You forget to step around the screen and look out at the real world.

To live in tempo is to look out the window, to look fearlessly at what is true in this very moment. To live in tempo is to live a life of action based on that clear sight. When you stick to what you actually see, you see that there is only ever one thing to be done, and you can always do that one thing perfectly. People miss out on this blatant easiness about things because they do not

19. David Mallett, "After the Fall" on *Parallel Lives*, Flying Fish Records, 1997.

make the distinction between the inside of their own skull and the real world.

You have probably noticed that the inside of your skull is a wildly unpredictable place; you have very little say over what floats down the stream of consciousness next. To take your own thoughts too seriously then, and to believe them at every turn, makes for a turbulent ride.

The good news is that we can direct our minds, rather than having our minds direct us. Often we are told that in order to succeed we must "follow our dreams." Better advice would be that in order to succeed, we must wake up from our dreams. To live in tempo, we must disbelieve our usual inner rambling about past and future and choose to take, over and over again, the one and only action available to us right now.

THE RELIGIOUS IMPULSE

A S SOON AS YOU BEGIN TO TAKE THE INNER power of music seriously, you look around and see something obvious: wherever religious practice is, there is music. It is exceedingly rare to find a religious service that does not involve music on some level. The presence of organized sound is one of the few common external markers — perhaps the only one — in religious practice across the planet, and it has always been so. The history of music before its use in collective ritual is essentially speculation; the two are practically inseparable. It is impossible to ask many questions about what religious practice is before you start running into music.

(Curiously, it is also difficult to listen to much music before you start running into the language of religion. Read the fatuous liner notes that accompany many recordings of the canon, and you find all sorts of "pantheon" and "divine inspiration" talk. Or, if you prefer, witness the not-quite-yet-iconic performers on *American Idol.*)

So the question for us is: what do music and spiritual practice have in common? What is the essence underlying all spiritual practice that music in some way mirrors? What is the connective tissue between the two?

We have all felt the possibility that there is a true impulse behind all the various religions, one that has been badly distorted and covered up in various ways by each of them. We do not have to be "religious" in the usual sense to inquire about this impulse. If it exists, it is a basic gesture of the intuitive faculties, a movement towards a kind of knowledge about things that nonetheless cannot be known. Thus it necessarily involves paradox on the deepest levels. On the one hand, it must be impossible to describe in literal language; if that were possible, we would have the description down by now. On the other hand, it must be extraordinarily simple, satisfying, and available to everyone. For if it is not available to everyone and does not satisfy everyone who actually follows through with it, then it is not a true answer to the human question. How can music help guide us toward this inner shift?

We know that music offers us an escape from ourselves. We can say, "I lost myself in that music." And the self that we lose is the reflective self, the self that is not engaged in real life. It is the self that sits at a distance, sculpts the résumé, thinks about what others think of us, and always feels either much better or much worse than everybody else. It is the self that is trapped in constant comparison. That is why it feels so good to lose the self for a minute or two in music. When it goes away, there is nothing left but peace. We feel as if we are touching the whole of life, because, of course, we are. The part of us that blocks the whole, the part of us that carves life up according to our own personal likes and dislikes, has stopped its work for a moment.

But music is by no means the only way to access this loss of self. Loss of self is also the real pleasure in sex. In the moment of orgasm, the *petit mourir* — the little death, the complete giving up of everything for an instant — there is a blindness and deafness towards all that separates you from spouse or stranger. Loss of self is also the joy of drinking — abandoning the grating anxieties of self-consciousness for an hour and smiling at the color of a wall or the tone of a voice you suddenly notice because you have stopped talking to yourself. To quiet that inner prattle of the mind, we turn every day to the television, the internet, the movie theatre, a meal out, dancing, shopping. Through these activities we enter the cool, dark tunnel where the voice of the reflective self can't reach us. We say that we engage in them with abandon, and that is true; through them, we abandon reflection. All our attention is absorbed by something else, and for a moment, thankfully, it is not turned in on ourselves. We touch something like oblivion, and it feels good.

So there are plenty of other tipping points into the loss of self besides music. Yet listening to music stands out as one that is not destructive when practiced to excess. Music is the only activity I just named that will not injure our well-being or our checking account when overindulged. Music is a sustainable access point to the loss of self, a legal and harmless drug. When the piece of music is over, you do not — well, at least not in the figurative sense — have to pay the piper.

And yet, while it may not be out-and-out destructive, music is still temporary. No matter how complete a reprieve music grants us from the weight of self-consciousness, the reprieve always comes to an end. So we are stuck; we have the impulse to lose ourselves, yet when we try, we are always deceived. Self-consciousness always returns. Frustration with this incessant return is the beginning of the religious impulse.

For the religious impulse is also the impulse to lose the self, but to lose it in a permanent way. It is the urge to escape the self, not by covering it up with a temporary drug, but by dismantling it altogether. The "self" that is dismantled through spiritual practice is the private way each of us perceives and interprets reality, a private way driven by body chemistry, genetic makeup, emotional habits picked up from parents and teachers, and all the accidental quirks of the individual personality. That personalized way of seeing things is like an optical lens, one that distorts our vision of the world. The desire to lose the self is the desire to see reality as it is — without this lens.[20] So all spiritual growth necessarily involves a kind of loss, a dropping, a shattering of that lens. To give up your self in this sense is to gain the world. To drop the partial view is to gain the whole.

This is why even saying something like "the religious impulse is the loss of self" is relatively useless. Mature religious practice doesn't speak about itself at all. It can't speak about a self to lose, for there is no self

---

20. As Albert Einstein said: "A human being is a part of the whole called by us 'the universe,' a part limited in time and space. He experiences himself, his thoughts and feelings, as something separate from the rest — a kind of optical delusion of his consciousness. This delusion is a kind of prison for us, restricting us to our personal desires and affection for a few persons nearest to us. Our task must be to free ourselves from this prison." Quoted in Jack Kornfield, *A Path With Heart* (New York: Bantam Books, 1993) 288.

left to say that it is lost. So on the one hand we might call it going beyond reflection, or we might just as well call it total reflection; that is, the mind looking down on itself and seeing itself for what it is, a vantage point badly limited by time. The mind willingly lays down its received perspective as one among an infinite variety. "Loss of self" is just a metaphor for this nameless experience that brings us into fuller contact with truth. Truth, in this sense, is simply what is left over when we stop telling ourselves our private stories about life. Obviously, then, anything one person says about truth will be partially untrue.

The taboo of the religious impulse is that the answers to our big questions — those questions we feel suffocatingly close to in the presence of death, birth, and other unanswerable mysteries — are simply not found in the mind. The mind cannot contain — cannot, in the old sense of the word, *comprehend* or *embrace* — actual experience; it can only file away a representation of an experience, a memory, or a prediction. This gap between our mind and the flow of experience is the problem of time that music solves — or rather dissolves. But the mind cannot hang on to any answer that will hold up for long apart from experience. A refusal to accept this truth results in the kind of shallow religion we see on television and on the street corner, the kind that claims to offer "answers" as facts to be held in the mind. Practitioners of such religion are generally cranky because such beliefs are constantly being contradicted by the flow of life itself.

The best that spiritual teaching can ever do is serve as a kind of diving board in the mind, a place from which to jump out of the mind and down into real experience in real time. If you try to talk in words about what is found there, you cut yourself off from whatever you find. In practical terms the important thing is not what is found, but the finding.

So another way to describe spiritual practice is this: it is the constant admission that wordlessness is the first condition of truth. Music, when it brings us to loss of self, brings us a step closer than religious language ever can, for spiritual truth is by definition beyond words. It is a terrible paradox. Religious stories the world over have had to hint at this silent alchemy in roundabout ways.

In the Jewish story of the Garden of Eden, for instance, the absence of the reflective self is the meaning of nakedness. Adam and Eve are naked in the garden, but have no consciousness of themselves as being naked. Nakedness represents the pre-self-conscious state into which everyone is born. Eventually, the ability to divide reality arises; that is, the ability to call some things "good" and some things "bad" — represented by the famous tree of the knowledge of good and evil. Making such distinctions generates a false sense of self in the mind. Suddenly, there is a sense of "me" to whom things can appear good or evil. That "me" can then turn in upon itself and call itself good or evil. Where before there was only one aspect to human existence — direct experience — now there are two. (Lest we miss this point, the snake, whose tongue is forked in two, is the first to mention the possibility of knowing good and evil.) This separate, imaginary self lodged in the mind must then impose some protection between its self and the rest of the world; thus the famous fig leaf. Adam and Eve's donning of the fig leaf is an image for our usual cowardly response, our tendency to separate ourselves from life rather than live it.

In the Zen Buddhist tradition, the student asks the teacher, "What is Buddha-nature?" The teacher replies, "Go wash your bowl." Christ's students ask him, "How do we enter the kingdom of heaven?" He says, "Give a kid a cup of cold water." *Outwards* goes the attention.

Our truth, the religious impulse tells us, is found in what we do, and never in our thoughts about what we do. This is the practical meaning in the Buddha's statement, "There is no self," or Christ's statement, "Love your neighbor as yourself." (i.e. "don't respect the distinction between other and self," i.e. "There is no self.") Get yourself out of the way and see what happens. What will happen, no one can say. Thus there is always an element of danger in the religious impulse. When it comes to the transformation of the individual, the only completely true doctrine is experience.

Experiencing this loss of self directly helps us make sense out of dusty old religious phrases like "newness of life." Newness of life is not something that zaps us from the outside, something magical. It is actually the complete opposite of magic. It is choosing to see time with a scientific accuracy, choosing to see that you have absolutely no control over what happens from minute to minute. You see the newness that is always coursing through life, with or without you.

The religious impulse, then, is a kind of active agnosticism. It is knowing that we can know nothing, but then deciding to push on the closed door anyway. The spiritual quest is not the quest to gain belief, but rather disbelief — disbelief in the self that rests in its own perspective as if it knew for certain. "Authentic growth," as one writer puts it, "comes from what we don't know."[21]

That silent leaning-into-the-unknown is the verb that flows behind all music, the essential activity in music that seems so much greater than us and that we can never put into words. And that verb, that elemental doing, is not separate from true spiritual practice. Music points to it, hints at it, and helps us on occasion to give up the burdensome daydreams of our pretended knowledge.

This essential motion of consciousness outward is the source from which "the right thing to do" always flows. All true ethics are simply a side effect of that impulse. When the self is lost, the line between self and other becomes blurred. And if you are really willing to take another person's viewpoint onto yourself, you will treat that person with kindness and truthfulness. It is a guarantee. If you listen clearly to others, you will behave with integrity, because you have integrated yourself into the whole fabric of things.

To lay down our false sense of self is, like music, simply an honest reaction to the fact of time, to the fact of our boundedness in time. Our sense of self, which is just a pile of adjectives, is going to vanish, every last bit of it, and probably sooner than we would like. The brain, with all its beliefs and answers, will decay right along with the rest of the body. So to go ahead and renounce

21. Michael Brown, in *The Presence Process* (New York: Beaufort Books, 2005) 19.

our private fantasy of who we are in exchange for the reality of what is[22] — this is the verb by which we come all the way alive.

The fundamental impulse toward which music points us is to live as a silent verb, to drop our useless playacting and simply be, to be real. That is why so many religious traditions involve bells. The single tone of a bell — ! — is in this instant a summary of all possible music. It is everything music is, condensed to an irreducible point. From high in the cathedral tower or couched in the lap of the meditator, the peal of a bell pronounces the unpronounceable verb of all music. The bell always says, "Yes!" "This is it!" "Do it now!"

Do what you have to do. The work you were born to do is either getting done, or it isn't. For love — it is such an abused word — has no existence apart from doing things. We tend to think of love as a feeling, then wait around for the feeling to come again. But we can only find love by doing. And when we do something with love, we see that none of our grandiose ideas about love were ever true. Love always takes us back to the humble, laughable THIS of our life.

Or as Thomas Merton, the monk who loved Bob Dylan, put it: "If you're constantly looking back to see if you're loving, well then, that spoils it. It's much better to just do something with this love, putting it into what you're doing, rather than reflecting back on yourself loving. Because if you reflect back on yourself loving, then you become artificially conscious of love and then it spoils it.

22. To borrow Krishnamurti's phrase; see also Robert A. Johnson, *Transformation* (San Francisco: Harper, 1991) 8.

Because it's got to be spontaneous. So the thing to do is . . . find something that suits you, that you can do in this kind of way, and then just go ahead and do it. And if it happens to be taking care of a cow or something, great."[23]

---

23. Transcribed from recording #176.1, "Sufism: Awareness of love in an awake heart." Recorded April 15, 1968. From the archives of the Thomas Merton Center at Bellarmine University and published by Now You Know Media as "Thomas Merton on Sufism." (Chevy Chase, MD, 2012).

SILENCE

THERE IS A LINE POPULARLY ATTRIBUTED TO Blaise Pascal: "All men's miseries derive from not being able to sit in a quiet room alone."

And if we are honest about the way we live, we will find that this is a true statement. Everything we think is amiss somehow boils down to a basic restlessness with ourselves that we all know from experience. Even if we believe ourselves to be the quiet and solitary type, if we sit still long enough we run into it — a deep-set fear of silence.

We fear silence because it allows us to hear the noise of our own annoyance at every circumstance. We are upset by the hot and the cold, the high and the low, the good and the bad. The grass is always greener on the other side of the fence; and in silence, we discover that we are the field on which the fence sits. Silence throws us headlong into our own perpetual indecision.

Perhaps we are indecisive because at heart we know that nothing we can choose to say is completely true. Nothing grasps the whole, nothing encompasses the total experience of life but silence. In silence we are up against the wall. If we try to say what we are, we cut ourselves in two. Silence, by contrast, is the only true philosophy; it accepts everything, it includes everything. And when we perceive this acceptance directly, the silence seems too much, too whole, too good to bear.

The purpose of music is to bring us to silence. In occasional flashes of grace, music's fullness empties us. As we listen, we become the silence in which music happens. We disappear. Music leaves a silent snowfall in the mind, and it is delightful.

Yet when the music is over, we stand invited to a still fuller silence, not just the inner silence of our private experience, but an immeasurable silence outside ourselves. Music has measured our now, played with it, sped it up, slowed it down. But when the sounds that measure time die, time itself goes away. Silence is the vacuum, the absence of time. It seems to us that we cannot escape time, yet silence is larger than time and stands behind it. Silence is what is left over when everything else is taken away; and from silence nothing can be taken away.

In silence we rest in the part of us that we always suspected was there but couldn't admit: the still center that remains perfectly unchanged by grief and joy, gain and loss. There is a part of us that is the same in the moment of birth as it is in the moment of death. If we are quiet enough, we can sink down into it. What is it?

We can only know it by its quietness. It can never have a name. But that inner silence, when it looks out at the world of time and change, somehow sees through appearances and recognizes itself. In silence, we look at this moment that every other moment has somehow added up to, and we have to smile at the deadly serious joke. Everything — the home, the family, the pets, the career, the friends, all the quirks of the world just as they stand today and perfect as they are today — all of it flowing, turning, on its way from silence to silence. Never again will it be as it is today.

The fact that you exist is the final miracle; there is nothing for which you must wait. Your life does not need anything that can be seen or heard or touched. Life is the seeing, the hearing, the touching. And it cannot add up to anything outside the quality of itself. Everything hinges on that. Life is life, and you are the empty space — the silence — through which it passes.

The only question, then, is whether or not you are able to hear this subtle music that is always sounding somewhere just behind things as they appear to be. Each day, that music is different. It cannot be captured, it cannot be written down, it cannot be stopped. Alone, again and again, you listen for it, a perfect music that can never be perfectly heard. Just now, in this irretrievable hour, where does the improvisation want to go?

We have been speaking for some time now about extraordinary states, about moments of great insight and meaning. But such moments appear unusual to us only when we are young and inexperienced at encountering them. After a while, such intensities appear normal, and we who have passed through them are left with something quiet, something supremely ordinary. At the end of the day, music wants to bring us home to that bedrock ordinariness where we can finally be at ease with whatever happens.

So I will be silent, and silence the pretense of book

and reader. I, the one writing these words in Nashville, wish you, the one reading them wherever you are, a musical life, a life in which you taste every minute for what it is. When you close this book, your life will be the way you touch the doorknob, the way you speak to the next person you meet. It is never anything else.

In other words, I wish you the courage to become what you have always secretly known yourself to be.

Acknowledgments

Very special thanks to Stan Link, Bryan Garner, Carl Smith, Lindsey Reymore, Peter Dayton, Kelby Carlson, and Evan Mack for reading the manuscript and making helpful comments along the way, but most of all, for countless conversations that served as a kind of draft for this book. To Mark Wait and Marianne Ploger, my gratitude for your constant support of my teaching, which wouldn't exist without you. To Christine Cote, for your steadfast belief in this book. To Lorin Hollander, for an evening lecture in a barn in Maine many years ago; though you won't remember me, I'm sure there is more of you in this book than I realize. To my parents, Johnny and Toni McGuire, for — literally — everything. And most of all, to Jennifer and Thomas: you make these things worth writing about.

FURTHER READING

In addition to the texts referenced in the footnotes, those interested in reading more about listening and its effects on the listener might explore the following books, articles, and resources:

Adyashanti. "Silence." In *Emptiness Dancing*. Boulder, Colorado: Sounds True, 2006. Pages 45–51.

Cone, Edward. *Musical Form and Musical Performance*. New York: W. W. Norton & Company, 1968.

Link, Stan. "Much Ado about Nothing," *Perspectives of New Music*, vol. 33, no. 1/2 (Winter/Summer 1995): 216–272.

Mathieu, W. A. *Bridge of Waves: What Music Is and How Listening to It Changes the World*. Boston: Shambhala, 2010.

(Ploger, Marianne) For updates on the teaching of Marianne Ploger, a systematic technical approach to musical listening, see www.plogermethod.com.

Small, Christopher. Musicking: The Meanings of Performing and Listening. Hanover, New Hampshire: Wesleyan University Press / University Press of New England, 1998.

ABOUT THE AUTHOR

Joshua McGuire is an award-winning opera librettist.
He currently teaches at
Vanderbilt University's Blair
School of Music.

♦ www.joshuamcguire.com

SHANTI ARTS
nature · art · spirit

Please visit us on online

to browse our entire book catalog,

including poetry collections and fiction,

books on travel, nature, healing, art,

photography, and more.

shantiarts.com

CPSIA information can be obtained
at www.ICGtesting.com
Printed in the USA
LVHW100554170519
618185LV00028BA/928/P